Bath Time

Written by Jane E. Gerver

Illustrated by Laura Ovresat

children's press®

A Division of Scholastic Inc.
New York Toronto London Auckland Sydney
Mexico City New Delhi Hong Kong
Danbury, Connecticut

Library of Congress Cataloging-in-Publication Data

Gerver, Jane E.
  Bath time / written by Jane E. Gerver ; illustrated by Laura Ovresat.
      p. cm. — (My first reader)
  Summary: A boy enjoys the look, feel, and smell of a bubble bath.
  ISBN 0-516-24677-1 (lib. bdg.)   0-516-25111-2 (pbk.)
  [1. Baths—Fiction. 2. Cleanliness—Fiction. 3. Stories in rhyme.] I. Ovresat, Laura, ill. II. Title. III. Series.
  PZ8.3+
  [E]—dc22
                              2004000234

1 2 3 4 5 6 7 8 9 10 R 13 12 11 10 09 08 07 06 05 04

Note to Parents and Teachers

Once a reader can recognize and identify the 46 words used to tell this story, he or she will be able to successfully read the entire book. These 46 words are repeated throughout the story, so that young readers will be able to recognize the words easily and understand their meaning.

The 46 words used in this book are:

a	feel	look	sparkle
as	feels	must	the
at	good	my	toe
bathtub	hair	new	too
bubbly	happy	nice	turn
clean	he	on	twice
dad	I	pours	wash
did	I'm	says	washing
dip	in	skin	water
dirty	is	smells	you
does	it	so	
father	job	soap	

I turn on the water.

I dip my toe in.

Dad pours bubbly soap.

9

I'm washing my skin!

My skin feels so clean.

The soap smells so nice.

My hair is so dirty.

I must wash it twice!

My father is happy.

21

22

He says, "Look at you!"

I did a good job.

I feel good as new.

I'm so clean I sparkle.

The bathtub does, too!

ABOUT THE AUTHOR

Jane E. Gerver is the author of many children's books, ranging from preschool board books to middle-grade fiction. She and her husband live in New York City with their young daughter, whose favorite activity is bath time!

ABOUT THE ILLUSTRATOR

Laura Ovresat can't remember a time when she wasn't drawing or painting. She attended art school in Chicago, where she lived for many years. Laura has created art for packages and illustrated posters and many books. She likes to spend her free time with her family and working in her garden. Laura lives in Eaton Rapids, Michigan, with her husband, her two daughters, a dog, and a cat.